My Princess Collection

Snow White

Love at First Sight

Book One

For more Disney Press fun,
visit www.disneybooks.com

Chapter One

Hello, I'm Snow White. I live an enchanted life as a princess with my husband, the Prince. But this was not always so.

My father died when I was very young, and my stepmother, the Queen, raised me. Though life wasn't always as wonderful as it is now, I wasn't unhappy living with her. What I didn't know was that the Queen was very jealous of me.

My job was to do all of the cleaning. I often sang while I worked.

One morning, I noticed someone watching me. It was the Prince! He had heard my singing and had stopped to find out where the music was coming from.

I stared into his eyes as I sang. Suddenly, I felt very nervous, and I ran inside.

Then, he called out to me. I stepped onto the balcony and kissed one of my doves and sent it down to him. It landed on his shoulder and delivered my kiss. Even though I didn't know who he was, I knew it was love at first sight for both of us.

Later, I wandered throughout the castle, thinking about him. I hoped he would return soon. I even dreamed we would get married and live happily ever after.

Chapter Two

The next day, the Queen's royal Huntsman invited me on a walk through the forest. We walked a long way, farther than I had ever gone before. I sang to myself as I picked flowers and made friends with the woodland animals.

Suddenly, I saw a dagger in the Huntsman's hand.

"I can't do it, Your Highness," he confessed, dropping the knife. "The Queen is jealous of you. She'll stop at nothing. Run away, hide, and never come back!"

I knew I was in great danger.

Chapter Three

I ran away, deep into the forest. I was very frightened. Before long, it was nighttime. It seemed as if scary monsters with bony arms were trying to grab me! And creatures with glowing eyes were watching me from the trees! I ran and ran until I collapsed from fright and exhaustion.

When it was finally morning, I realized that
the bony arms were really tree branches, and
the glowing eyes in the darkness belonged to
my animal friends. They had watched over me
all night long. I was no longer scared. But I
was very tired and needed to find a place
where I could rest.

Chapter Four

My animal friends led me through the woods to a sunny clearing. There I saw a charming little cottage.

I knocked at the door. There was no answer, so I turned the handle. The door opened! What a strange house, I thought. There were seven little chairs and seven little beds upstairs with

the names Happy, Sneezy, Sleepy, Dopey, Bashful, Doc, and Grumpy carved on them.

I also noticed that the place was a terrible mess. I wondered if seven little children lived here—with no one to look after them.

I decided to help the children by cleaning up. When they returned to see their house neat, they'd surely let me stay. My animal friends helped me sweep and dust and scrub until the cottage was spotless.

Chapter Five

After I had finished cleaning, I was very tired. I fell asleep in one of the beds.

A voice woke me suddenly. "Why, it's a girl," someone said.

I opened my eyes and sat up. The "children" weren't children, after all. They were seven little men!

I told the Seven Dwarfs who I was and I
explained what the wicked Queen had tried
to do. "If you let me stay," I said, "I'll wash
and sew and sweep and cook."

"Cook!" they shouted. "Hooray!"

We had so much fun that night. I made a delicious soup for dinner, which everyone really enjoyed.

After dinner, some of the Dwarfs played music while I danced with the others. I also sang a song about the Prince. It made me smile just thinking about him.

Chapter Six

The next morning, I had breakfast with the Seven Dwarfs before they went to work in the diamond mine. I kissed each one of them good-bye as they left. Grumpy was the last to leave.

"Remember, don't let nobody or nothing

in the house!" he cried.

That made me smile. I realized that even though Grumpy was gruff, he did care about me.

After they left, I decided to bake some gooseberry pies for the Seven Dwarfs. Just as I was putting the finishing touches on one, an old woman passed by the window.

"Making pies?" she asked. "It's apple pies that make menfolks' mouths water." And she held out a big red apple.

I had promised the Dwarfs that I would avoid strangers, but I didn't think the old woman seemed dangerous at all.

Suddenly, a flock of birds flew down and knocked the apple from her hand. "Go away!" she cried to the birds.

I rushed into the cottage and got her a glass of water.

"Because you've been so good to poor old Granny," she said, "I'll share a secret. This is a magic wishing apple. One bite and all your dreams will come true."

I thought of the Prince. Could we finally be together? I raised the apple to my lips and wished that my prince would come to take me away. I took a bite. Something was wrong. I felt dizzy. Then, I couldn't stand and I fell to the floor.

Chapter Seven

The apple made me fall into a long, deep sleep.

The following spring, I awoke. I was lying on a beautiful bed, surrounded by flowers. The Seven Dwarfs were there—and so was the handsome Prince!

My animal friends had saved me. They got the Dwarfs and led them to the cottage. There the Dwarfs saw the Queen running away. They chased her up a mountaintop and away forever!

Then, the Prince had found me and he woke me with a kiss. As I rode off with my true love, I realized that all of my wishes had come true.